PAPERCUTZ™

MANOSAURS

#1 "WALK LIKE A MANOSAUR!"

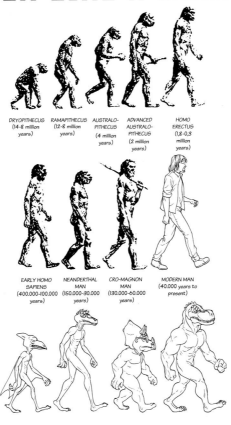

STEFAN PETRUCHA — WRITER

YELLOWHALE STUDIOS — ARTISTS

MANOSAURS CREATED BY STUART FISCHER

PAPERCUTZ™

NEW YORK

#1 "Walk Like a Manosaur!"
Inspired by the MANOSAURS comicbook series created by Stuart Fischer.
Man-Comet co-created by Stefan Petrucha and Maia Kinney-Petrucha.

Stefan Petrucha – Writer
Yellowhale Creative Studio s.r.l. - Rome/IT
Marcello De Martino – Artist
Roberta Pierpaoli – Inker
Francesca Vivaldi – Colorist
Maryam Funicelli, Dawn Guzzo – Letterers
Stefania Bitta – Studio Supervisor
MANOSAURS logo design – JayJay Jackson
Martin Satryb – Design/Production
Jeff Whitman – Assistant Managing Editor
Jim Salicrup
Editor-in-Chief

ISBN: 978-162991-813-6 paperback edition
ISBN: 978-162991-814-3 hardcover edition

Papercutz books may be purchased for business or promotional use.
For information on bulk purchases please contact Macmillan Corporate and
Premium Sales Department at (800) 221-7945 x5442.

Printed in Korea
November 2017

Distributed by Macmillan
First Printing

MANOSAURS, REGROUP!

PTOR WAS SO *HEAVY*, I'M TOO DRAINED TO BE ANGRY!

MUST... LICK WOUNDS...!

I JUST REALIZED, NO MATTER WHAT HUMANS THINK OF US, WE'RE *NOT* ALONE.

BECAUSE WE HAVE EACH OTHER?

MORE THAN THAT! LOOK UP! IT'S AS IF, FROM ACROSS THE AGES, OUR ANCESTORS LOOK DOWN ON US!

THE *DEAD* WON'T HELP YOU ANY MORE THAN THE HUMANS!

IN A FEW MOMENTS, YOU'LL BE *JOINING* THOSE BONES!

"WAIT. WAIT.

"WAIIIITTTTT.

"WAIT."

WATCH OUT FOR PAPERCUT

Welcome to the post-historic, premiere MANOSAURS graphic novel, based on the comicbook series created by Stuart Fischer, written by Stefan Petrucha, and illustrated by Yellowhale Studios, from Papercutz—those amateur paleontologists dedicated to publishing great graphic novels for all ages (not just the Jurassic!). I'm Jim Salicrup, Editor-in-Chief and Fossil Fool, here to ramble about MANOSAURS and Papercutz…

While dinosaurs existed between from about 230 million years ago up until about 65 million years ago, MANOSAURS are a relatively new thing. They were first discovered in 1993 in two MANOSAURS comicbooks, #0 and #1. The MANOSAURS are created by Stuart Fischer, a man I've met just a few times, and who I mostly remember for his connection to *Mutt and Jeff* and his *Green Lantern* ring. Stuart's a clever guy, and the idea of creatures that combine the relative strengths of humans (intelligence) and dinosaurs (strength) is so good, you have to wonder why no one else ever thought of it. I'm hoping this new incarnation of MANOSAURS becomes a huge hit, not only because I want Papercutz to publish as many super-successful graphic novels as possible, but I secretly want my original MANOSAURS comicbooks to become valuable ($$) collector's items.

Guiding the MANOSAURS back to comicbook life is none other Stefan Petrucha, a writer who has been with Papercutz since the beginning, writing such titles for us as NANCY DREW DIARIES, POWER RANGERS, RIO, MICKEY'S INFERNO, and HOTEL TRANSYLVANIA. Stefan has written all sorts of comics over the years, such as *The X-Files*, *Donald Duck*, *Meta-4*, *Lance Barnes*, *Post Nuke Dick*, *Squalor*, and was even nominated for a Bram Stoker Award for the graphic novel, *Kolchak Night Stalker: Devil in the Details*. Stefan's also written tons of books, including such YA series as *Timetripper*, *Rule of Won*, *Split*, plus *Dead Mann Walking*, *Ripper*, *The Shadow of Frankenstein*, as well as novels starring *Captain America*, *Deadpool*, and *Spider-Man*. For a peek at his latest Papercutz project, check out the preview of HOTEL TRANSYLVANIA on the following pages.

Believe it or not, this isn't the first time Papercutz has published a graphic novel series with talking dinosaurs. Take a look at the preview pages from DINOSAURS, by Arnaud Plumeri and Bloz, to get a taste of what that fact-filled series is like. Before I get too carried away, let me remind you that you can find out about all the available graphic novels we publish at papercutz.com. There may even be a peek at MANOSAURS #2 "The Horrific, Dreadful, Awful, Terror of Thesaurus—The Thing with Many Names!" So on that note, allow me to say good-bye, farewell, so long, adieu, aloha, adios, ta-ta!

Thanks,

STAY IN TOUCH!

EMAIL: salicrup@papercutz.com
WEB: www.papercutz.com
TWITTER: @papercutzgn
INSTAGRAM: @papercutzgn
FACEBOOK: PAPERCUTZGRAPHICNOVELS
REGULAR MAIL: Papercutz, 160 Broadway, Suite 700,
    East Wing, New York, NY 10038

Don't Miss HOTEL TRANSYLVANIA #1 "Kakieland Katastrophe," available now at booksellers everywhere!

TYRANNOSAURUS REX

LET'S TAKE A LOOK AT THIS SULLEN LITTLE DINOSAUR…

HEY, GUYS, CHECK OUT WHO'S TURNED UP! IT'S THE LITTLE RUNT!

HI, LITTLE RUNT! YOU'RE UGLY, YOU KNOW THAT?

…IT DOESN'T LOOK LIKE HE HAS AN EASY LIFE…

SO, UGLY DUCKLING, YOU'RE WALKING AROUND LIKE A GROWNUP?

YOU DO KNOW YOU COULD GET YOURSELF INTO SOME TROUBLE?

;GRUMMBLLLE;

GET OUT OF MY TERRITORY, YOU UGLY, LITTLE RUNT!

YUM! A JUICY LITTLE FLEDGLING!

WAAAH!

FLAP FLAP FLAP

SUCH TRAGIC SCENES. BUT SOON THE TABLES WILL TURN!

AT ADOLESCENCE, OUR LITTLE DINOSAUR WILL LOSE HIS FEATHERS…

?

AND WILL GROW AND GROW INTO A TERRIFYING TYRANNOSAURUS REX!

ROAR

A DIFFICULT CHILDHOOD… COULD THAT BE THE REASON FOR T. REX'S NASTY TEMPER? IT'S A MYSTERY!

ROOO OAR

WHY'S HE SO MEAN?

TYRANNOSAURUS REX

MEANING: TYRANT LIZARD KING
PERIOD: LATE CRETACEOUS (68-65 MILLION YEARS AGO)
ORDER/ FAMILY: SAURISCHIA / TYRANNOSAURIDAE
SIZE: 35-50 FEET LONG
WEIGHT: 11,000 POUNDS
DIET: CARNIVORE
FOUND: NORTH AMERICA

T. PLUMERI & BLOZ-REX

TRICERATOPS

MEANING: THREE-HORNED FACE
PERIOD: LATE CRETACEOUS (68-65 MILLION YEARS AGO)
ORDER/ FAMILY: ORNITHISCHIA/ CERATOPSIDAE
SIZE: 30 FEET LONG
WEIGHT: 20,000 LBS.
DIET: HERBIVORE
FOUND: NORTH AMERICA

AT HOME WITH THE PTEROSAURS

VELOCIRAPTOR

ONCE UPON A TIME, THERE WAS A SLIGHTLY STUPID *PROTOCERATOPS*...

THE DROMAESAURIDS! THE DROMAESAURIDS!

SAY WHAT? SAY WHO? WHY? YOU'RE LEAVING?

...WHO DIDN'T KNOW THAT THE MOST FAMOUS *DROMAESAURIDS* WERE...

RAPTORS!

HE DISCOVERED THEIR FAVORITE WEAPON RIGHT AWAY!...

HOLY COW! YOU DON'T CUT YOUR TOENAILS OFTEN ENOUGH!

VGH!

AND THEIR FAVORITE WAY OF CHASING: STALKING...

PUFF...

GO AWAY!

PUFF... HELP!

PUFF...

...TO EXHAUSTION!

THAT'S GOOD! HE'S DONE FOR-- LET'S EAT!

ONCE UPON A TIME, THERE WERE SOME SLIGHTLY STUPID *VELOCIRAPTORS*...

?

?

?

..WHO DISCOVERED THAT *TARBOSAURUS* WAS A LAZY GUY.

NO FAIR! WE DID ALL THE WORK!

SSANKS, DUDES!

GIVE US BACK OUR MEAT!

VELOCIRAPTOR

MEANING: SWIFT THIEF
PERIOD: LATE CRETACEOUS (75-70 MILLION YEARS AGO)
ORDER/ FAMILY: SAURISCHIA/ DROMAEOSAURIDAE
SIZE: 7 FEET LONG
WEIGHT: 30 LBS.
DIET: CARNIVORE
FOUND: MONGOLIA, CHINA

DINOSAURS #1 "In the Beginning…" is available at booksellers everwhere.